THE
CHRISTMAS
CHEEKY CAT
meets Santa!

Written by Rippon Pawa
Illustrated by Amy Harwood

For Amiya
and Nikhil

Once upon a time during the festivities of Christmas, there was a cat called GINGER.

Ginger loved Christmas time and really wanted to meet Santa Claus to tell him what present she wants.

She was a
Cheeky Cat!

One day while Ginger was going for her walk,
she saw Santa's Grotto in the park.

Ginger thought,
"this is my chance
to meet him and tell
him what I want
for Christmas."

Ginger saw that the front door
was open to the Grotto.

When Ginger saw nobody was looking, she started...

running, running, running, running,

to the front door and got

one paw

inside, when suddenly an elf
jumped out and said

"GINGER,
you Cheeky Cat!

You aren't allowed
in Santa's Grotto!
Before Santa sees you, you
better turn around
and go home!"

So Ginger turned around
and went home.

The next day, Ginger was going for her walk again
and saw Santa's Grotto was still there.

This time, Ginger saw the window was open
in the Grotto.

When Ginger saw nobody was looking, she started...

running, running, running, running,

to the open window and got
one paw,
then two paws
inside, when suddenly the same elf
jumped out and said

"GINGER,
you Cheeky Cat!

You aren't allowed
in Santa's Grotto.
Before Santa sees you, you
better turn around and
go home!"

So Ginger turned around
and went back home.

On Christmas Eve, Ginger went for another walk and saw Santa's Grotto again.

This time, Ginger saw the back door was open to the Grotto.

When Ginger saw nobody was looking, she started...

running, running, running, running,

to the back door and got

one paw,
then two paws,
then three paws

inside the door, when suddenly the elf jumped out and said

"GINGER, you Cheeky Cat!

You aren't allowed in Santa's Grotto.
Before Santa sees you, you better
turn around and go home!"

So Ginger turned around and went home.

The next day was Christmas and Ginger wasn't sure what to do. She really wanted to meet Santa Claus but wasn't allowed to.

Ginger thought about being a good cat and staying at home.

Ginger heard something outside.

Santa Claus was dropping presents at Mia and Nicky's house. They were the children that lived next door.

Let me try to meet him one more time

she thought.

So Ginger climbed over the fence and
jumped into Mia and Nicky's garden.

Ginger went very slowly at first and when nobody was looking, she started…

running, running, running, running,

to Santa's sleigh.

This time Ginger got
one paw,
then two paws,
then three paws,
and finally four paws
into the sleigh, but where was Santa?

Santa was eating a tasty mince pie, as he was returning back to his sleigh.

Just then, the elf jumped onto the sleigh, where Ginger was sitting.

The elf was just about to make Ginger go home,
when Santa said

Ho ho ho, hello Ginger, you cheeky cat. What can I give you for Christmas this year?

Ginger couldn't believe it, Santa Claus knew her name.

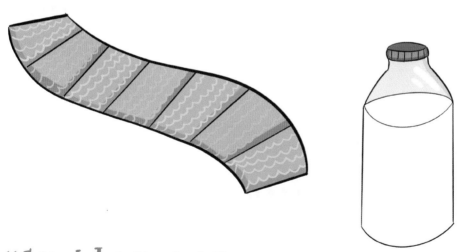

"Can I have a new scarf please Santa and lots and lots of milk?"

said Ginger.

Santa gave a big smile and said
"Ho ho ho, of course you can!"

As if by magic, Santa and Ginger were in Ginger's house, where he gave her a beautifully wrapped present, which she opened straight away.

Ginger put her brand new scarf on and drank
the milk Santa put in her saucer, before jumping
onto Santa's lap for a cuddle.

And from that Christmas on, Santa always made sure
he had a present for Ginger...

and lots and lots of milk with it.

Ginger really was
a Cheeky Cat!!!

Rippon Pawa

This is the third book of The Cheeky Cat series, following on from *The Cheeky Cat* and *The Cheeky Cat meets the Queen*. These books have meant so much to me personally as they started from the imagination of my daughter. Will there be a fourth instalment, who knows? However, I hope you and your little ones continue to enjoy these books. Stay Cheeky!

Amy Harwood

Amy Harwood is a freelance Illustrator based in Southampton, UK. She creates imagery inspired by nature and animals, and she also teaches art workshops in her studio and online – *amyharwood.com*

Other titles from the author:
The Cheeky Cat
The Cheeky Cat Meets the Queen

Printed in Great Britain
by Amazon